Jules Verne's

Twenty Thousand Leagues Under the Sea

Retold For Kids

(Beginner Reader Classics)

Max James

KidLit-O Press

www.KidLito.com

Table of Contents

ABOUT 4

PART I 5

    CHAPTER 1: A RUNAWAY REEF.................................6

    CHAPTER 2. THE GOOD AND BAD.............................8

    CHAPTER 3: AS MASTER WISHES.............................10

    CHAPTER 4: NED LAND 13

    CHAPTER 5: AT RANDOM!..16

    CHAPTER 6: AT FULL STEAM...................................18

    CHAPTER 7: AN UNKNOWN WHALE 21

    CHAPTER 8: "MOVING INSIDE THE MOVING THING" 24

    CHAPTER 9: THE TANTRUMS OF NED LAND 27

    CHAPTER 10: THE MAN OF THE WATERS 29

    CHAPTER 11: THE NAUTILUS 31

    CHAPTER 12: EVERYTHING THROUGH ELECTRICITY.............33

    CHAPTER 13: SOME FIGURES 35

    CHAPTER 14: THE BLACK CURRENT 36

    CHAPTER 15: AN INVITATION IN WRITING 40

    CHAPTER 16: STROLLING THE PLAINS 44

    CHAPTER 17: AN UNDERWATER FOREST 47

    CHAPTER 18: THE OCEAN IS ALL WE NEED 49

    CHAPTER 19: VANIKORO...50

    CHAPTER 20: THE TORRES STRAIT 51

    CHAPTER 21: SOME DAYS ASHORE 54

    CHAPTER 22: THE LIGHTINGING BOLTS OF CAPTAIN NEMO .56

    CHAPTER 23: TROUBLED DREAMS 59

    CHAPTER 24: THE CORAL REALM 61

PART II 64

    CHAPTER 1: THE INDIAN OCEAN 65

    CHAPTER 2: A NEW PLAN FROM CAPTAIN NEMO 66

    CHAPTER 3: A PEARL WORTH TEN MILLION 67

    CHAPTER 4: THE RED SEA 70

    CHAPTER 5: ARABIAN TUNNEL..............................73

    CHAPTER 6: THE GREEK ISLANDS 75

CHAPTER 7: THE MEDITERRANEAN IN FORTY-EIGHT HOURS 78
CHAPTER 8: THE BAY OF VIGO 80
CHAPTER 9: A LOST CONTINENT 85
CHAPTER 10: THE UNDERWATER COALFIELD.......................89
CHAPTER 11: THE SARGASSO SEA 91
CHAPTER 12: BALEEN WHALES 94
CHAPTER 13: THE ICE BANK 96
CHAPTER 14: THE SOUTH POLE 99
CHAPTER 15: ACCIDENT OR INCIDENT? 102
CHAPTER 16: SHORTAGE OF AIR 105
CHAPTER 17: FROM CAPE HORN TO THE AMAZON.............108
CHAPTER 18: THE DEVILFISH 109
CHAPTER 19: THE GULF STREAM..113
CHAPTER 20: TO EUROPE AGAIN 116
CHAPTER 21: A MASS EXTINCTION.......................................117
CHAPTER 22: THE LAST WORDS OF CAPTAIN NEMO 122

CONCLUSION **126**

About

KidLit-o was started for one simple reason: our kids. They wanted to find a way to introduce classic literature to their children.

Books in this series take all the classics that they love and make them age appropriate for a younger audience—while still keeping the integrity and style of the original.

We hope you and you children enjoy them. We love feedback, so if you have a question or comment, stop by our website!

PART I

CHAPTER 1: A RUNAWAY REEF

1866 was a strange year for scientists. Even for sturdy captains of sturdy ships, and government officers all over the world. Something so big happened at sea that it raised everyone's eyebrow. What could have happened?

In July, ships had left to the dark blue sea like any other day. But they came across an "enormous thing" in the water. It looked like a long spindle or a very wide rod. Sometimes it gave off a bright light. It glowed and sometimes it disappeared. It was also bigger and faster than any whale, even a blue whale, and it moved like a steam train.

Captain Baker believed the thing was a runaway reef, a small piece of land that moved in the water. He was about to draw it on a map and give it a name when two water streams shot out of the reef, 150 feet into the air! If it was not a reef then the only other explanation could be that it was a new animal. It was a weird large creature that hid deep underwater. And it gave everyone trouble when they were at sea.

The creature had a sharp instrument on the front of its head. It used the instrument to cut through other ships at sea and sink them. Because every ship was in danger, no one wanted to travel across the sea. Instead, everyone wanted to get rid of it!

CHAPTER 2. THE GOOD AND BAD

I was here in New York to explore. I am an assistant professor and scientist at the Paris Museum. And I arrived from France not too long ago. Although New York welcomed me, I could not stop thinking about the new creature. Every newspaper had written about it. It was like a puzzle and no one could put the pieces together. What was this "enormous thing" I wondered?

Every scientist had said that it was only a large sea animal. And that it was undiscovered, no one had ever seen anything like it. I think that it was a large narwhal. A narwhal is a type of whale that has a very long and thin horn on its nose like a unicorn. So I decided to write about it.

The American government had read what I wrote about the mystery of the giant narwhal. They were preparing a battleship to hunt and chase it down. The name of the ship was the Abraham Lincoln and its commander was Commander Farragut. They sent a letter to me three hours before the Abraham Lincoln were to depart for the sea. The letter read:

To Mr. Pierre Aronnax
Professor of the Paris Museum,
Fifth Avenue Hotel
New York, NY

If you would like to board the Abraham Lincoln, the American government would accept you as the ambassador of France. Commander Farragut has a cabin for you. We hope that you accept our offer and we will be setting a course for the Northern Pacific Ocean.

Sincerely,
J.B. Hobson, of the Navy

CHAPTER 3: AS MASTER WISHES

I wanted to help the world solve the puzzling mystery of the narwhal. I accepted the offer to help the Americans look for it. After all, the only way ships would be safe at sea is if the Abraham Lincoln chased down this troubling monster and rid the world of it!

"Besides," I thought, "I can bring back the narwhal's large ivory tusk for the Paris Museum."

"Conseil!" I yelled.

"Conseil!" I yelled again. Conseil was a very thin and small boy who went on every journey with me. He was also my loyal servant. His name means counsel.

"Conseil!" I yelled a third time.

Conseil entered the room.

"Did master yell for me?"

"Yes, my boy. Get my things ready; get your things ready, we're leaving. Get all the clothes; just pack it in, hurry. Just squeeze it in," I said.

"As master wishes."

Conseil packed all of our shirts and suits, but he could not fit the fossils I brought from my museum. We left the fossils behind then we took a car and came onto Bowery Street, turned on Katrin Street, and stopped at Pier 34. It was the 34th dock that had the Abraham Lincoln waiting for us.

An officer stood to greet us on the board walk. The Abraham Lincoln had a blackish blue color from all the dirt. Its where the ocean's waves could not reach it. Conseil and I were filled with excitement, knowing we will soon be aboard a mighty battleship.

"Professor Pierre Aronnax?" the officer asked me.

"Yes, the only one," I said. I asked him if he was Commander Farragut. He was! He kindly walked us onto the Abraham Lincoln, then to my personal cabin.

"Is the pressure high?" Commander yelled to his crewmen!

"Yes! It's very high," the crewman, who was covered in soot, yelled back to Cammander Farragut.

"Go ahead, then!"

The engine blew steam from every pipe and the steam was blacker than night. Then the propeller sent the Abraham Lincoln out into the water. It was 8:00 o' clock in the evening and we ran full steam into the Atlantic Ocean.

CHAPTER 4: NED LAND

The Abraham Lincoln was ready to fight. It had hand harpoons, sharp arrows, and duck guns with exploding bullets on board. And it had cannons that could fire miles out to sea. As for the crewmen, they wanted to harpoon the monster and to sell the meat.

I learned that Ned Land, an old friend, was on board! He was very tall, and about 40 years old. He was a good seaman, and he was strong, almost too strong.

He was worth the whole crew all by himself just with his throwing arm. I can only say that he was like a telescope ready to fire a harpoon at any moment.

On the evening of June 25 Ned Land and I had an interesting conversation.

"Ned," I asked him, "how can you still not believe it?"

He slapped his forehead and closed his eyes, and then he finally said:

"Just maybe, Aronnax."

"But Ned! You're the best whale hunter I know," I said.

"Any talk of monsters living at sea is nothing more than a fairy tale. I've seen many whales, but not a single one can cut through an entire ship."

"Well I believe the ship stories," I went on, "it must live deep in the ocean."

"Why do you say that?" Ned Land wondered.

"Because it takes a lot of strength to live there, the pressure is so high it could crush anything."

"Bosh!" he claimed.

"It's true! If the monster lived 10 meters underwater it would feel 10 times the pressure than the surface. At 100 meters it would feel 100 times the pressure and at 1,000 meters it would feel 1,000 times the pressure!" I said.

"Fire and brimstone!" Ned Land put it.

Ned Land never believed in anything until he saw it with his own two eyes. He was also like a knight on the quest to get rid of a dragon. But instead of a dragon it was a giant narwhal. Either he would slay the giant narwhal or the giant narwhal would slay him.

CHAPTER 5: AT RANDOM!

The next day the Abraham Lincoln reached the waters of the Pacific Ocean.

"Open your eyes! Open your eyes!" all the crewmen were shouting.

We watched the surface of the water every minute of every day and every night. We passed the Hawaiian Islands, the area where the monster was seen last.

I stared and stared some more until I almost went blind. Conseil stared at my side. Ned Land pretended not to even look at the water, but his vision was still better than ours. He stared at water for a living.

Eventually, the ship steered off course, made sharp turns, and stopped at random to search for it. Then it searched every beach of Japan and America. It took one year. And we found nothing! We found no giant narwhal, no runaway reef and no monsters.

On the night of November 12 1867, huge clouds gathered near the moon. Conseil and I were on deck.

"Searching for this monster is a waste of time, my boy," I said.

Exactly at the moment when Conseil opened his mouth to say a word or two, we heard a voice from behind:

"There it is! There it is!"

CHAPTER 6: AT FULL STEAM

It was Ned Land shouting and he had spotted a mass in the waters. The entire crew of harpooners, workers, and sailors rushed over to Ned Land.

My heart was pounding. The water is difficult to see at night, but the sea was lit up by a long light in the shape of an oval and glowed on and off like a light switch.

It appeared to be the monster's glow and it was the brightest at the center. The light circled around the Abraham Lincoln, at twice our speed! We were all frightened. It was so very fast.

"What is it, master?" Conseil whispered.

"Maybe," I said, "it's a giant electric eel—"

The monster shot out water into the air from its blow hole!

"It's a whale!" I yelled.

Then it suddenly sped away.

"Full steam! Toward the monster!" Commander Farragut turned to his crewmen.

The Abraham Lincoln was one of the most powerful American ships ever built. The Abraham Lincoln picked up speed.The ships engine roared so loudly that it made me nervous.

"Conseil," I said, "we might blow ourselves up if the ship keeps this speed."

"If that's what master wishes!"

Suddenly, the giant narwhal stopped in its underwater tracks. It glowed brighter and brighter.

"Bah!" Commander Farragut said, "load the cannons!"

"Maybe it's tired," I thought.

I saw Ned Land draw back his arm, and hurl a dangerously sharp harpoon with all of his might. The harpoon made a clunk then bounced off the giant narwhal's back. Its glow quickly disappeared. Then two powerful water streams shot out of the giant narwhal again and onto the deck of the Abraham Lincoln. Five sailors fell over the rails, and I was hurled into the sea!

CHAPTER 7: AN UNKNOWN WHALE

I'm a good swimmer, with two kicks I came back up to the surface. I knew how to stay calm in the water.

"Help!" I shouted, swimming toward the Abraham Lincoln.

My clothes were heavier than lead. The Abraham Lincoln was leaving; its lights disappeared. I thought I was done for.

"Help!" I shouted once more. My mouth was filled with water and I was slowly sinking. But then, out of nowhere, a set of hands pulled me up to the surface!

"If master leans on my shoulder, master will swim easy."

"You!" I said. "You!"

"Myself."

"You were thrown overboard?"

"Not at all, I followed you master," the boy thought following me into the sea was only natural. I couldn't believe it!

We tried to keep each other afloat as long as possible until a new boat or ship came by. It was impossible and exhausting! We slowly started sinking together now.

Suddenly, something banged against us! It felt like a small island underneath our feet and kept us afloat. Then we heard a familiar voice, and saw a shape walking toward us in the moonlight.

"Ned! You were thrown overboard!"

"In person, and still after the giant narwhal," he said, "I was thrown into the sea but I was luckier than you and landed on this floating island."

"A floating island?" I wondered.

"You're standing on the giant narwhal. But the giant narwhal isn't a narwhal or a floating island!" Ned Land said.

"What do you mean?"

"My harpoon couldn't cut through it, it's made of steel!"

We stomped our feet and heard an empty bang underneath. It was true; the giant narwhal was made of metal! We were standing on a machine built by human hands and one which could travel underwater. It was hard to believe, but we were on it!

What would we find inside? What kind of strangers would live in it?

Suddenly, a steel hatch flipped open! Then eight gigantic men came out of the hatch, their faces were like masks, and they dragged us down into the unknown machine. They captured us at lightning speed. And they were holding knives and daggers.

CHAPTER 8: "MOVING INSIDE THE MOVING THING"

The walls inside of this unusual 'thing' were lit by an electric glow. It was the same glow we had seen observing from the Abraham Lincoln. The men dragged us in to a small prison holding room.

"Brimstone!" Ned Land cried.

A man entered who had thick black hair, a long mustache, bright eyes, powerful muscles, and wide shoulders. The man's eyes were strangely spaced; they were too far apart. He was the commander.

"Master, you should tell our story," Conseil said.

Conseil had a good idea, so I explained everything starting with our names: Professor Pierre Arranox, Conseil and Ned Land. Then I explained our jobs and how we arrived at sea. The man could not understand a single word and his stares were empty and blank.

Then Ned Land started our story all over again! He used wilder hand gestures and a louder voice. Nothing worked. Then Conseil retold it in German, French, and Latin!

"These are bad men!" Ned Land yelled.

"Quiet!" I said, "don't get angry, they might hurt us."

"That's the problem of not knowing every language, master," Conseil said.

A servant entered with food and clothing. He laid some jackets and sailor pants down onto the floor. They were crafted from a strange fabric that might have come from the inside of seashells.

After we changed into our new clothing we sat down at the small wooden table. The servant had brought colorful fish and vegetables! I noticed there was something carved in the wood, "MOBILIS IN MOBILI," it was Latin, and it means "moving inside the moving thing."

CHAPTER 9: THE TANTRUMS OF NED LAND

"We have to escape," Ned Land said.

"There is nothing we can do," I said.

"You're wrong!" Ned Land shouted. "We can break out of here!"

"Keep your voice down," I said, "it's impossible, we're under water!"

"It's not professor," Ned Land went on, "all we have to do is fix things around here."

"We can kick the guards, servants and the captain off and into the sea!" Conseil whispered.

We waited for hours on end for an opportunity. Ned Land was growing angrier the longer we were imprisoned. He was like a beast, pacing back and forth. He was hungry then started growling and shouting!

That's when the servant walked in and Ned Land dashed to him! He jumped onto him and threw him down! He was holding him by the throat. Conseil was already trying to loosen the powerful grip of Ned Land's hand.

"Calm down, Mr.Land! And you, the professor, listen to me!"

CHAPTER 10: THE MAN OF THE WATERS

The commander had spoken. And in our native language!

"Gentlemen," the commander said, "I speak French, German, Latin and I could have easily replied. Now release my servant."

The commander's voice was strong and clear, Ned Land let the servant go.

"You are my enemies, Professor Arronax, Mr. Land, and Conseil," he said, "you have been chasing me throughout the sea in your battleship."

"We don't have to chase you now that we know this thing isn't a giant narwhal," I said.

"I've cut ties with every land, and every country. I am a man of the waters. Your country shall chase me no matter what."

After we calmed ourselves, Captain Nemo offered an unusual proposal:

"I will allow all of you to be free aboard my ship," he went on, "you can walk, eat, and observe as you wish. But you can never leave now that you've discovered my secret."

 "By thunder!" Ned shouted.

 "One question, sir," I wondered, "what do we call you?"

"Simply Captain Nemo, and you are my prisoners aboard the Nautilus."

We were all frightened by our new situation, but we couldn't do anything to change it. His crewmen were too strong to fight and it was impossible to swim across the ocean. Our only choice was to accept Captain Nemo's offer.

CHAPTER 11: THE NAUTILUS

Captain Nemo gave me a private tour around the Nautilus. I wanted to know every marvel a ship like the Nautilus hid. I followed him to an enormous library lit by electric light.

It was like a palace. There were at least 7,000 books on the shelves in every language. There were some about science, outer space, and history and were all treasures to my eyes.

Then we walked over to the lounge which housed a museum. Paintings of the seas and sculptures of sea shells were all over the place. They were worth millions of Francs. I was in a state of joy becausenNot even a museum in Europe owned such a collection from the sea.

I thanked him then said:

"You must love the sea."

"Yes, it's my home," he kindly told me to take a seat.

CHAPTER 12: EVERYTHING THROUGH ELECTRICITY

I sat as Captain Nemo spread his arms across a wall of all the gauges, instruments, and levers attached to it. They were tools to measure temperature, location, and the pressure inside of the ship.

"I've never seen a few of these instruments before, captain," I said.

"Yes, those are the ones that control a powerful force on the Nautilus," he warned me, "electricity!"

"But sir, how can this ship have so much of it?" I wondered.

"The sea has all sorts of metals that help the Nautilus generate enormous amounts of electricity."

"But that's not all, professor, if you would please follow me," he added.

Captain Nemo then led me to the Nautilus's stern. He explained how he was able to send a telegram to the Nautilus through a wire which connected to him to control the ship. It was able to follow him anywhere he went. It was a miraculous machine filled with secrets to the brim.

CHAPTER 13: SOME FIGURES

I found out everything about the Nautilus! Its cylinder and cigar shape gave it its quick speed and its ability to turn. It collected water in the walls which reinforced the steel plates as it submerged down to astonishing depths! To rise back to the surface it released the water. In fact, the walls had the resistance of stone blocks.

The Nautilus had only one problem. It could only store two days worth of air for the entire crew.

Captain Nemo loved the Nautilus as if it were his own flesh and blood. To my delicate surprise, Captain Nemo was the sole engineer, the builder, and the captain! It had cost 2 million Francs to build. He was an infinitely rich man, and could pay off the French national debt. All I could say to Captain Nemo was, "Bravo Captain!"

CHAPTER 14: THE BLACK CURRENT

If one league is three miles across the sea, the amount of water the planet holds can make a sphere of sixty leagues across! The sphere would weigh three quintillion tons or three billion billions. Captain Nemo was the first commander in the world to explore its greatest depths.

We made our way through the central hallway which led to a set of metal steps. I passed through the hatch, and arrived at the top of the Nautilus. I glanced over the ocean. The metal on the outside of the Nautilus were like the scales of a reptile.

The sea was magnificent and the sky was clear. There was no land, island, or Abraham Lincoln, only the vast blue horizon.

"Professor, whenever you're re Nemo said below.

I took one last look at the sea then cloⁱ hatch.

"We herby begin our voyage of exploration under water," Captain Nemo said, "and now here are the charts for our course. The lounge is at your disposal professor. I must take my leave."

I still wondered what kind of character Captain Nemo was. Conseil mentioned that he is one of those Galileo types of men, a pioneer of science which the world had not accepted yet. I couldn't say. One day it would do us some good to find out.

I looked over the old and browned charts. Our next destination was a Japanese river called the Black Current.

"Where are we heading?" Ned Land asked.

"My friends," I said to them, "we are fifty meters below sea level and safe aboard the Nautilus."

aster says it, then it must be!" Conseil said.

t was a treacherous waterway to be on so I decided to not mention it to my friends.

"I haven't seen anyone around lately! Could they be electric too? How many men are on board 10, 20 or 100?" Ned Land said nervously.

"Ned you must get rid of your notionto take over the ship. It's impossible. Besides, we are inside one of the greatest inventions in the world!" I said.

"It's the beginning of the end," he said.

The lounge was separated from the sea by two layers of thick glass and thin metal sheets. We stared into the large windows. The water was like liquid light. All sorts of sea creatures swam across as if the Nautilus was invisible.

Bright ones, yellow and gold ones, and we saw almost every color we could think of. Some swam too fast and others gently. We saw Japanese eels and salamanders that were six feet long and had sharp little eyes.

CHAPTER 15: AN INVITATION IN WRITING

On November 16, I found a note in my room. It was written with Old English style. The note read:

Professor Aronnax, passenger on the Nautilus, November 16, 1867

Captain Nemo invites Professor Aronnax on the hunting trip which will take place tomorrow on the Crespo Island forests. Captain Nemo hopes nothing will delay the professor from attending.

From: Captain Nemo, Commander of the Nautilus.

I brought the note to my friends.

"A hunting trip!" Ned Land shouted.

"And he has an island?" Conseil added.

"So this means the commander goes ashore?" Ned Land said, "sweet, sweet, land. We're saved!"

"If Captain Nemo does go ashore," I said, "then he'll no doubt choose an empty far off island. We'll be deserted if we make a plan to escape."

The next morning I entered the lounge and talked to Captain Nemo about something which had bothered me.

"Captain, why is it that you cut ties from every country, and own forests on an island?"

"These forests are mine, professor," he replied, "they don't hold lions, tigers, deer, or elephants. These forests are actually underwater forests."

"Underwater forests?"

"Yes."

"We shall be hunting in these underwater forests?" I wondered, "with rifles in hand?"

"Yes, with rifles," he said.

I looked at him as if his mind was not in place. He must be crazed with an illness or disease I thought.

"Professor, you must not make snap judgments. You might think I was insane, talking about underwater forests," he said, "but listen to me."

"We are going to hunt at the bottom of the sea," he went on, "we have special suits that can withstand the pressure, but also collect air, and light the darkness by turning carbon dioxide into light."

"And the rifles? They aren't gunpowder?"

"They are air rifles," Captain Nemo said, "and shoot little glass capsules."

I returned to Conseil and Ned Land.

"Prepare yourselves, my companions. We are going hunting on the bottom of the sea!"

CHAPTER 16: STROLLING THE PLAINS

We found ourselves in a large room near the very bottom of the Nautilus. Hanging on the walls were dozens of diving suits and oddly shaped rifles, tanks of oxygen, and everything for a stroll underwater.

The suits had large round helmets made of copper and tubing. The material felt flimsy and loose. What sort of material were they and would they protect us from the pressure?

"Will you risk it?" Ned Land asked Conseil.

"Where master goes, I go," Conseil replied.

"That's right, my boy," I said and threw a helmet to both Conseil and Ned Land. The captain and one of his crewmen also put on a suit. The crewman was gigantic and looked as if he had the strength of Hercules.

The room slowly filled with sea water. It was dark, but the lights on our helmets lit the way. We stood frightened for a moment, not knowing what adventure waits at the bottom of the sea.

A powerful sun ray hit the seafloor. It lit objects 100 meters away! We were 30 meters deep.

Vast plains of sand seemed endless like liquid curtains. I noticed sparkling rocks and green sea plants, and prickly coral covering the ocean floor. Some were pink and black and others reflected light. The sand had trails and paths carved out by the water's currents and breezes.

Conseil looked at me, and we stopped at the beautiful sight. We were afraid to walk and crush the thousands of life living underneath our feet, comb shells, hammer shells, coquina seashells which jump, top-shell snails, red helmet shells, angel-wing conchs, and baby crabs!

There were schools of milky white fish, and octopi that let their tentacles float over our heads. Jelly fish appeared as if they were in a slow vibration through. We saw glowing creatures, and creatures that blended in.

As we walked the water deepened and the sun light from above slowly faded. We were 100 meters below the surface now. What were we hunting for if not the sea creatures and schools of fish nearby? I wondered.

CHAPTER 17: AN UNDERWATER FOREST

We entered a dark underwater forest. It had plants similar to trees which gave the forest its darkness and shadow. The branches weren't normal branches, they did not poke us instead they rose straight up into the air.

Then we walked on large blocks of stone which were covered in green algae and by other small plants. They were ancient ruins created by the earth. It was an underwater kingdom!

Plants attached to everything. They covered grains, pebbles, seashells, stone, and husks because they had no roots and moved freely across with the gentle water breezes.

At the bottom of the seafloor everything was calmer. But near the surface waves and water bumped and crashed into each other so powerfully it could wreck a ship.

A gigantic spider had blocked our path. It was impossible to scream and be heard. It stared with its beady eyes; I wondered if it could jump like a spring in the water? It scared the light out of my suit.

Captain Nemo signaled his gigantic crewman. The crewman took one swing at the body of the spider with his rifle. It flipped onto its back, its legs curled up and then its eyes closed.

Captain Nemo aimed his rifle and fired off a shot at a dark moving thing nearby. It was a magnificent sea otter and had to be worth a high price. It was an extremely rare creature, on the verge of extinction. The gigantic crewman picked up the animal and carried it on his shoulder. Then we set off again to finally reach the Nautilus safely.

CHAPTER 18: THE OCEAN IS ALL WE NEED

The next morning, November 18, the Nautilus floated on the surface of the sea. Captain Nemo commanded twenty crewmen to pull up a large fishing net. Inside of the net were scores of angelfish, clownfish, and other strange types of fish. It was at least 1,000pounds.

 "The ocean is all we need, professor., Captain Nemo said.

"Yes," I said, "after all it was the ocean that created it all."

"Salt!" Captain Nemo said, "it was salt that created it all. It accumulated and built the continents and the land," then he disappeared into the hatch.

CHAPTER 19: VANIKORO

Captain Nemo placed a finger over the map and said one word:

"Vanikoro."

"We've reached it?"

"Yes, professor."

"But isn't Vanikoro known for ship disappearances?"

"It's a peaceful and calm place for ships to rest."

The island Vanikoro was a sight of creation, lavish with sun rays and turtles that lay their eggs, and birds that nested in the branches of the tall trees.

The Nautilus passed through the sharp coral reefs of Vanikoro without any trouble; we noticed the graveyard of French ships from 1785.

CHAPTER 20: THE TORRES STRAIT

On January 1, 1868 Conseil joined me on the platform while the Nautilus collected air to replenish the tanks. We were near the Torres Islands.

"Will master allow me to wish him a happy new year?" the gallant lad said.

"Thank you Conseil," I said, "I hope the new year will be truly happy aboard the Nautilus. How long do you think we can go on without land?"

"I don't know master, I can live without land, meat or wine, but Ned Land cannot."

How far will we travel with the captain I wondered?

On January 4, the Nautilus approached the Torres Strait. It was one of the most dangerous passages in the world because of its knife-like coral and shores of savage inhabitants. The passage was wide but had rocky and coral obstacles that would challenge even the strength and speed of the Nautilus.

The Nautilus moved at a steady pace. I took a seat near Captain Nemo who manned the wheel and steered the Nautilus.

"That's one rough sea!" Ned Land said, "Captain Nemo must be a mad man to traverse this course!"

If the coral had scraped any inch of the Nautilus we would sink.

I was suddenly thrown to the ground. The Nautilus was caught by the very last leg of the passage! The walls retained not a single scratch, they were so powerful.

Captain Nemo had given my friends and I the permission to visit the Torres Islands while he solved the problem with the help of his crewmen.

We were all excited to be on land finally, especially Ned Land, "Meat! Meat! Meat!" he repeated to himself quietly. He had the desire to hunt every animal on the island he could spot.

We got in a longboat which the Nautilus carried and set off toward the Torres Islands. As we rowed toward the shore, I worried we would encounter savages.

CHAPTER 21: SOME DAYS ASHORE

Pine and palm trees were mixed together. Ned Land spotted a coconut tree. He cracked open a coconut and drank the milk inside.

We found another weird fruit. It was green and large. We decided to cook it. The inside of it tasted like bread! The flavor reminded me of an artichoke.

We swept through the forest collecting as many palm cabbages, coconuts and bread fruit as possible. Ned Land noticed all of the parrots cackling and flying from tree to tree.

"We need something with four paws!" Ned Land cried, "those parrots are only appetizers."

Ned Land had caught a beautiful piglet for us to grill and we returned to the shore.

Suddenly, a small stone sped by and landed in front of our feet. It frightened Ned Land; he accidentally let go of the piglet and it ran wildly back to where it came from.

CHAPTER 22: THE LIGHTINGING BOLTS OF CAPTAIN NEMO

We stared at the trees from where the stone flew.

"Apes maybe?" Ned Land whispered.

"Nearly," Conseil said, "savages!"

"Head for the boat, my boy, and Ned!" I smiled and was already off, moving faster than light toward the longboat and the sea.

At least twenty appeared with bows and arrows.

Stones and arrows rained down on us. We rowed back to the Nautilus and hurried to find Captain Nemo.

"Captain!" I shouted.

"Captain!" I shouted again. He turned and grabbed my hand, "we've brought back a horde of savages!"

"Have no fear professor," Captain Nemo said, "the Nautilus could withstand all of their attacks, even if there were 1,000 of them!"

Hundreds of them on canoes surrounded the Nautilus! They were ready to enter the hatch.

"Let them enter!" Captain Nemo yelled.

"But we'll be eaten alive!" I cried.

"Come with me, professor."

We came underneath the first hatch. A savage had touched the rails of the hatch and some invisible force made him fly backward. He howled like a coyote. It happened to ten more and all ten were sent running.

Ned Land was curious and touched the rails. He flew backward and cried:

"Brimstone! I've been struck by a lightning bolt!"

The Nautilus was set free by the tides, and we took possession of the sea again. We gathered speed and we left underneath a hail of arrows. The Nautilus was a remarkable invention which protected us like a sacred ark.

CHAPTER 23: TROUBLED DREAMS

On January 16 the Nautilus drifted through a school of glowing jellyfish while Captain Nemo carefully watched the horizon with a spyglass. He also periodically paced back and forth, stomping his feet.

His hands were clenched tightly by his sides, and his teeth were half showing. I almost had not recognized him. He had grown angrier the more he stared at the horizon's shore.

"Professor Aronnax," Captain Nemo said, "I must temporarily imprison you and your companions once more."

He led us to the prison room and closed the electric door behind us. Lunch was served for us in the same way. We felt the boat sway as the Nautilus picked up speed.

After lunch we grew weaker each breath and my eye lids began to close. A powerful drowsiness came over us. We fell into a deep sleep.

CHAPTER 24: THE CORAL REALM

The next day we awakened with headaches. We were carried back to our rooms as well. And we were no longer near the shore on the horizon.

Captain Nemo was tired and his face was glowing a bright red fleshy color.

"Professor Aronnax," he said, "I need your help, you are a doctor aren't you?

"Yes, but how did you know?" I replied, "before the Paris Museum I received my degree in medicine."

"One of my men is sick; I would like you to help him."

"Let me see this sick man," I demanded.

He led me to the man's room. He was lying in bed and couldn't move because he was wounded.

The man's head was wrapped in linen and covered in blood. The wound was too severe and the bandage should not be disturbed. I asked how he had received such a terrifying wound, but Captain Nemo wouldn't answer. I told him that nothing can save this man.

"Nothing?" Captain Nemo cried, tears were rolling down his eyes.

"Would you and your companions like to make an underwater dive today?"

"We're yours to command," I said.

"Please go put on your diving suits."

By 8:30 our suits were on. I recognized the coral realms! The coral realms are large groups of coral that had tiny sea animals attached to a stony and brittle stem.

The coral forest expanded into a kingdom of organ-pipe coral, stony coral, star coral, and fungus coral. I noticed one of the crewmen carrying something oblong and dark. He set it down then dug a hole

"Of course!" I thought. Captain Nemo kneeled, and then the crewman buried the wounded man underneath this magnificent coral world.

END OF THE FIRST PART

PART II

CHAPTER 1: THE INDIAN OCEAN

Let us begin the second part of our journey. Right now everything that has happened has only showed one side of Captain Nemo. He was a lost scientist, and a genius who used the Nautilus to escape society. The wounded crewman had raised too many questions that may never be answered.

We continued our stay on the Nautilus and stumbled upon a sea of milky waves; they were white as they crashed into each other. In the sky we saw the colorful glow that formed a faint aurora borealis.

CHAPTER 2: A NEW PLAN FROM CAPTAIN NEMO

On January 28th I observed mountains in the distance. We were in the Bengal Bay of the East Indies.

"Ceylon Island" Captain Nemo said, "famous for its pearl fisheries."

"I would love to fish for a pearl, captain" I said.

"Then I hope you're not afraid of sharks."

I was frightened by the mere thought of sharks and their enormous jaws. It was difficult to breath simply knowing sharks lurked nearby. However, some of the pearls might be worth thousands of Francs!

CHAPTER 3: A PEARL WORTH TEN MILLION

The oyster bank was clear of fisherman and divers. It was still day light at the perfect diving spot where we surfaced and were preparing to dive for pearls.

We dove one by one off the platform and into the cold sea water. The life at the bottom were mostly edible duck clams, horrible looking crabs, water plants and frog crabs that were a part of Hindu cuisine. I observed the giant crab, discovered by Darwin; it can eat coconuts off a tree and break them open with the strength of its pincers.

We strolled along an underwater trail until we stopped at a gigantic oyster clam, two meters wide, and was sitting in a crack between two large stones. Captain Nemo stuck his dagger in between the shell's mouth to prevent it from closing. He lifted a pearl the size of a coconut! Its value had to be at least ten million. He put it into his sack.

Suddenly a black shadow moved near Captain Nemo.

It was a shark! A huge wave knocked Captain Nemo down and hurled him away leaving him open to the predator's enormous jaw!

Ned Land swam over and placed himself in between Captain Nemo and the shark. Then he thrusted his harpoon into the massive white bellied shark and saved Captain Nemo.

After we returned to the Nautilus and revived Captain Nemo said:

"Thank you, Ned. You saved me in the land that I am to this day a native!"

CHAPTER 4: THE RED SEA

Ceylon Island disappeared on the horizon. We were continuing our journey across the Indian Ocean. On February 6th the Nautilus reached the Red Sea at full speed. It was the great Roman Empire that once used these ancient waters as a place for trading goods.

Ned Land had grown frustrated. Steam was ready to come out of every breathing hole on his body. We wondered if we would ever see France, Europe or our homes again. But for now we cannot take any action to overthrow Captain Nemo. He had not done anything wrong. We knew him as a hero until this point!

I spent hours in the lounge. I watched the new and unique specimens of the Red Sea such as spongy coral and armored fish! The spongy coral grew into various shapes resembling fingers, circles, ovals, baskets, paws, tails, and gloves! There were silver scaled fish, triggerfish, parrotfish, fish with yellow heads and mullets, blue fins, yellow fins, and gold fins.

"The Red Sea is a miraculous sight," I said.

"Its named after its red color."

"Where does it get such a color?" I wondered.

"From the small algae and plants that release red pieces into the water."

"That is an excellent source," I said.

"The sea holds many secrets," Captain Nemo went on, "but now you must prepare yourself to be in Mediterranean waters in two days."

"In two days?" I said, "that's impossible, we would need to circle around Africa!"

"That's right, professor Aronnax," Captain Nemo smiled then told me he knew of a secret tunnel.

CHAPTER 5: ARABIAN TUNNEL

"An underwater tunnel!" Ned Land shouted, "I've never heard of one!"

"Mr. Land," I said, "but have you heard of the Nautilus until this time?"

"We'll see," Ned Land said.

The propellers stopped abruptly. The Nautilus sank along the walls of the Arabian coast. Captain Nemo never took his eyes off the compass.

Suddenly, waves were pulling us into a dark hole in the wall; we were hurled toward it like an arrow. The Nautilus went along at a blazing speed; my heart would not stop pounding. Then we rushed out of the tunnel.

Captain Nemo let go of the wheel and turned to me:

"Professor, the Mediterranean."

We sped through the tunnel so quickly that Ned Land and Conseil had not the faintest idea. They were sleeping in their rooms.

CHAPTER 6: THE GREEK ISLANDS

On February 12ᵗʰ, the Nautilus surfaced in Mediterranean water.

 "Bosh!" Ned Land said, "so it's true, there is a tunnel that connects the two seas."

"Only a ship like the Nautilus would be able to discover such things," I said.

"Well then, this is the perfect time to talk, professor."

"About what?" I wondered.

"We are fairly close to home," he said.

"Ned, my friend," I said, "answer honestly, are you sorry that fate has cast you into Captain Nemo's hands?"

Ned Land crossed his arms.

"Honestly, I'm glad we have done this voyage, but to have done it, it has to finish. And so far it has not finished."

"It will finish, Ned" I said.

"When?"

"Only time can tell."

"But we are here! In Europe, now! Tomorrow we might be back in China or some strange island!" he shouted.

"I understand Ned, you just look out for the chance we can make our escape, but if we fail, Captain Nemo will never forgive us."

On February 14th I decided to study the Greek islands and its native fish. Suddenly, I was startled by the sight of a man swimming across in the window.

"A man! A castaway!" I shouted, "we must rescue him at all cost!"

Captain Nemo remained calm and walked up to the window. He signaled the man with his hand as if he knew him.

"That's Nicolas, he's a well known diver throughout the Greek Islands."

Captain Nemo filled a chest with so much gold worth at least five million. Five crewmen hoisted it to the surface. Then I heard footsteps on the platform and the longboat being casted out to sea.

CHAPTER 7: THE MEDITERRANEAN IN FORTY-EIGHT HOURS

The fresh air and the sight of rugged mountains, orange trees, cacti, and pine trees was calming. The tuna fish were swimming in the shade of the Nautilus to escape the sun rays. Many snails latched onto the bottom of the Nautilus!

On the rocky seafloor there was blooming flora: sponges, sea cucumbers, jellyfish and other plants that gave off faint glows. The sea was more purplish and darker than the Red Sea.

The Mediterranean Sea had many sunken ships. It was a site where captains and sailors had lost a battle or were swept away by the ocean waters and into the basin. I had a small glimpse into the ruins of the Temple of Hercules. It was buried by the water long ago. Forty-eight hours later, the Nautilus resurfaced on the Atlantic Ocean.

CHAPTER 8: THE BAY OF VIGO

The Atlantic Ocean is fed by the world's largest rivers: St. Lawrence, Mississippi, Amazon, and Niger. The Nautilus covered 10,000 leagues in three months.

Our short trip across the Mediterranean had not given us anopportunity to plan an escape.

Ned Land was staring at me:

"We'll do it this evening."

My body stiffened. I couldn't answer; I was the only one who wished to stay. But I couldn't go against Ned Land, my dear old friend; it was not in my personality.

"This evening, we'll be right next to the Spanish shore," Ned Land said, "you promised you would help, professor, I'm counting on you."

"We'll do it at nine o'clock when Captain Nemo and the crewmen should be asleep," he kept on, "the night will be cloudy, and the winds will be blowing directly to the shore. Everything we need is in the longboat, Conseil has already agreed to the plan."

"The sea will be rough," I said.

"It's worth risking."

I hoped for more time to talk it over. I avoided Captain Nemo at all costs, afraid that if he found out he would leave us stranded in the ocean.

I visited the lounge for the last time. The museum had all the art and treasure I could imagine. I also didn't want to leave before the greatest discovery; to find out whether Captain Nemo was a hero or a villain.

Captain Nemo appeared behind me.

"Professor, listen carefully, I'll give you a piece of history that will help you resolve your unanswered question."

I froze, I couldn't say a word. Was he aware of our escape plan?

"I'm listening captain."

"We are currently in the Bay of Vigo. On October 22, 1702 English ships arrived onto the shore. An enemy had heard of these ships and attacked, and when English Admiral Renault fought, he saw that the wealth and treasures were falling into the enemies' hands. So he buried and spread the treasure all along the waters."

"How could this possibly help me?"

"Well, Professor Aronnax," he replied," all that's left is for you to unravel the mysteries of this bay."

Captain Nemo stood up and invited me to follow him. The lounge was dark, and crewmen were busy clearing barrels and trunks. Out of these barrels spilled massive amounts of gold, silver, jewels, and sand.

"Did you know professor," Captain Nemo asked, "that the sea contained such wealth?"

"I knew that it was only estimated, but no one knows the true value of all of the sea's treasures."

"I pick up what other men lose to the bottoms of the sea floors."

"I now understand where you're wealth comes from," I said.

"I put my good wealth to use professor; do you think I'm unaware of the suffering people and oppressed races living on this earth, poor people, and victims of society?" Captain Nemo said.

The next morning, February 19, Ned Land came into my room with a face of great disappointment.

"Well Ned," I said.

"Well, sir, the ship had stopped before it reached the shore."

The Nautilus was leaving Europe. Ned Land wept; we were 150 leagues away from the nearest coast.

CHAPTER 9: A LOST CONTINENT

"Professor, would you like to see the depths of the ocean on a dark night?"

"Very much," I replied.

"Are you sure? It will be a tiring stroll across an underwater mountain and for long hours," Captain Nemo said.

"I'm very curious," I said.

"Let's put on our diving suits."

We put on our suits and left the Nautilus. The waters were so dark that our lights only reached a few meters. No one else accompanied us.

So what were these vast plains that we were crossing? We walked for at least four hours, until the darkness had suddenly changed into a glowing white light. The glow was coming from a mountain. The top of the mountain may have been 250 meters.

We climbed rocks, broke tree trunks, and scared schools of fish as we moved toward the mountain. I leaped over black gaps that would swallow me if I fell in.

As the light came closer we saw a large collection of enormous rock walls which leaned on one another They were perfectly cut and shaped. They were like towers. There were actual structures at the bottom of the ocean! I saw them!

Every now and then, a huge antenna swam by or a pincer clamped and snapped nearby. Captain Nemo kept moving forward.

We stood at the base of the mountain when it released a gigantic explosion of lava. Where am I? I wished to speak.

Then Captain Nemo walked up to me. He scratched some letters on a black volcanic rock. He scratched this word:

ATLANTIS

No one believed Atlantis existed, yet there it was; the ancient land that was never found. I felt it! I climbed it. The 9,000 year old city was right under my nose.

For thousands of years the city of Atlantis rested on an island. The Atlanteans were great engineers and architects who built structures that were far more advance than the rest of the world. But the island had too many earthquakes and volcanic eruptions. The earth swallowed the island deep into the Atlantic Ocean.

By fate I was put on the mountain of Atlantis. As we walked forward we crushed old animal bones that once roamed the fields. They were turned to stone and still held there animal shapes.

We walked together around the plains that glowed from crystals. We stayed in this place for one hour, thinking about the gigantic inhabitants who lived in warlike towns and could raise blocks of stone into the air! Then after the hour on the lost continent, it was time to return to the Nautilus.

CHAPTER 10: THE UNDERWATER COALFIELD

When I told my boy-servant where I had taken a stroll he had not listened to a single word I said. He was too distracted by the bony blackish fish in the window. What kind of lad was he? Does he not take interest in ancient cities and strong, intelligent giants? It was a useless effort; no one will ever believe me.

The next morning the Nautilus surfaced. I stepped out onto the platform. The air was dirty and it was hard to breath. It was dark and I couldn't see much of anything. We were in a lake surrounded by walls at least two miles away.

"Where are we?" I asked Captain Nemo.

"In the very heart of an extinct volcano," he told me, "which has all the metal in the world to run my Nautilus."

Conseil, Ned Land and I took great pleasure in strolling across the volcanic land. We stretched our legs on the sandy beaches of the crater. To our surprise, there were animals roaming about, a few birds and bee hives and the views were soft on our eyes which put us to sleep for a while. After our earthly nap we boarded the Nautilus and navigated out of the shores back into the waves of the Atlantic Ocean.

CHAPTER 11: THE SARGASSO SEA

On February 22, we spent time in the strange Sargasso Sea in the north Atlantic. Surrounding this huge mass of water were currents that circled around similarly to a giant whirl pool.

Captain Nemo planned an experiment in the Sargasso Sea to test the strength of Nautilus at some of the greatest depths imaginable. I took a seat in the lounge.

Under the Nautilus's powerful thrust, we began to sink. The captain and I watched the needles of the pressure gauges slowly rise. Soon we reached a depth that was not livable. There were no schools of fish or any kind of life. Then the needles in the pressure gauges started swerving back and forth.

The instruments indicated a depth of 6,000 meters. The Nautilus continued to sink. After an hour we were at 13,000 meters. Then down to a depth of 14,000 meters. We saw black mountain peaks below us that could be as tall as the Himalayas!

"What an excursion!" I shouted. Traveling at such great depths had made my heart pound like it was going to race out of my chest.

"We must go back up, professor." Captain Nemo said, "it is a great risk each time the Nautilus faces such unbearable pressure."

"Hold on tight!" Captain Nemo smiled.

In four minutes, I was hurled onto the floor, the fins and propellers of the Nautilus were set to vertical and we shot upward with lighting speed! The view in the window was grainy, and we were pushed upward by so much water pressure that we surfaced like a flying fish into the air! We fell back into the sea which caused large waves to ripple through the ocean like a heavy raindrop.

CHAPTER 12: BALEEN WHALES

A baleen whale poked its nose into the window.

"Look! Look!" Ned Land cried, "it's approaching!"

"Oh!" he said, "it's not just one whale it's ten, no twenty! And I can't do a thing about it!" He yelled and pretended he had a harpoon in his hand.

"Ned," Conseil said, "why not ask the captain to hunt—"

Before Conseil finished speaking, Ned Land was gone! He ran up the hatch in search of Captain Nemo. When he found him and asked to hunt the baleen whales, they found themselves in a little argument.

"—they are destructive beasts who eat everything!" Ned Land yelled.

"But they are still unnecessary to hunt," Captain Nemo said.

Ned Land's anger and worry accumulated inside. After some time, Captain Nemo was convinced and he released Ned Land with a harpoon to hunt the whales. Ned Land's desire for his old life was burning in him like a wild fire, and Captain Nemo had put a little bit of water on that fire.

And as the days went on, so did Ned Land's attitude which grew worse and worse.

CHAPTER 13: THE ICE BANK

On March 14 was the first time we encountered icebergs on our voyage. They looked as dangerous as a canyon of rock. Ned Land had fished in the arctic oceans before so he must know his way about. The Nautilus stopped in front of a giant barrier of ice, as tall as 30 meters and as sharp as 200 knives.

"The ice bank!" Ned Land yelled, "listen professor, if the captain tries to go through the bank, we'll be done for."

"How do you mean, Ned?

"Walls were invented to frustrate scientists," Conseil said.

"No matter how powerful the Nautilus, after the wall there is only land that the Nautilus cannot trek," Ned Land said.

"How can we turn back?" I wondered, "the water is frozen solid behind us."

"We're trapped," he said.

"Trapped, how so?" Captain Nemo smiled.

"Well we can't move backwards, forward, or sideways. That's the very definition of trapped!" I said.

"Don't think the Nautilus can clear the ice?" Captain Nemo said.

"With only the greatest difficulty to your Nautilus," I replied.

"Oh professor," Captain Nemo said, "we shall reach the South Pole with the Nautilus!"

The hatches closed. Ten men grabbed picks and chipped away at the ice that was forming around the lower parts of the ship. We were set free.

And there was sea underneath the ice bank! We slowly submerged like an alligator into the freezing water. We bumped along the underbelly of the ice bank.

CHAPTER 14: THE SOUTH POLE

The next morning on March 19, we found the open sea. The air had a thick mist. We couldn't see anything around us, but the Nautilus could finally move with ease.

We were destined to discover and explore the South Pole as Christopher Columbus had explored the North American continent.

Captain Nemo checked the gauges.

"We made it," Captain Nemo said.

He let out a short breath. We launched the longboat with a couple of crewmen carrying equipment for ice climbing.

The soil on the island was volcanic and had the texture of rocky ice gravel.

"It's good that Ned Land didn't come along!" Conseil said.

"Why do you say that, my boy?" I wondered.

"Master, he would hunt all of these animals!"

There were magnificent seals and walruses all around. They were large and sleepy. One occasionally yawned into the air, but it was a roaring yawn. When these animals wanted to move they moved in little jumps. Their gentle features were amusing, soft limp eyes, and awkward poses.

"Well said my boy," I praised him, "and we know how much the captain dislikes huting animals that do no harm."

Dark grey clouds covered the sky. We climbed over the large lava rocks and onto a small peak where we could stand over the view of the vast sea. At the summit Captain Nemo said:

"Gentlemen, the South Pole."

He took out a long black roll of fabric from his sack and unrolled it. The letter "N" in gold was stitched on the flag's center. He turned toward the last remaining sun which was only a small sliver in the clouds and pleaded:

"Farewell, O sun!" he called, "let six months of night cover my new lands!" Then he drove the flag into the gravel.

CHAPTER 15: ACCIDENT OR INCIDENT?

By the next morning we had returned to the Nautilus. The polar star twinkled and the thermometer read -12 degrees Celsius. As for the seals and walruses they were trudging around the ice banks chasing away the birds.

It has been five months now since my friends and I were brought aboard by Captain Nemo. By now we had traveled at least 14,000 leagues: a greater distance than the earth's equator.

On this day, it was the first time the Nautilus tipped over onto its side. We were returning from the South Pole, under the ice bank. The couches were tossed around and everything slid to one side.

"What happened?"

"Brimstone!" Ned Land shouted, "the Nautilus finally did it, it's been struck!"

"You mean an incident?" Conseil asked.

"Yes!" Ned Land cried.

"No, sir," Captain Nemo said as he entered the lounge, "an accident."

"Are we in danger captain?" I worried.

"No we are only stranded," he said.

"May I learn what caused it?"

"An entire mountain top collapsed onto us!"

Captain Nemo had an ingenious plan to turn us upright again. The Nautilus had used the air tanks to balance itself.

We realized we were still surrounded by ice bergs and ice banks on every side except the southern side. So the Nautilus picked up speed and headed south.

"It's over with!" Ned Land mumbled then added, "as long as we get out of this arctic, I don't care where we sink to next."

At 6:25 in the evening the Nautilus had hit something which shook the whole ship frantically again.

"Professor, I'm afraid we have another turn of events this evening. An iceberg now closes every exit."

"We're trapped?"

"Yes, professor."

CHAPTER 16: SHORTAGE OF AIR

The entire Nautilus was trapped in a prison of ice. Ned Land's face was the color of an angry red bird; he banged his large harpooning fist on the table. The captain turned to all of us, with a regrettable face and said:

"Gentleman, crewmen, all of you must listen. We have 48 hours until the air reserve tanks will empty. We'll try cutting through one of the walls blocking the way."

Ned stood up.

"Captain," Ned Land said, "I'm ready to help with a pick," Captain Nemo reached his hand out to Ned Land.

"I'm counting on everyone's efforts; we will make it through," Captain Nemo assured us.

Everyone worked the southern wall of ice. Each wall was slowly moving closer together. It was one more danger that could instantly crush the Nautilus.

Hacking the walls away with picks hadn't accomplished much, the walls were too thick. The picks hardly broke through, not even 10 meters. We worked all day.

Captain Nemo stood silent for a moment and crossed his arms at his chest.

"Boiling water," he mumbled.

"Boiling water?" I wondered.

"We can raise the temperature around the Nautilus and break free."

After three hours we released steam water from the Nautilus's engine pipes and caused the thermometer to rise from -6 to -4 degrees Celsius. The Nautilus was 2 degrees warmer!

We were all stretched out on the ground barely conscious.

"Oh, if only I could give you the air in my lungs, master!"

Conseil squeezed my hand. I was turning blue and purple. Just then we felt a shift in the walls of the Nautilus. We fell into the sea through the 400 meter thick surface of ice which crumbled beneath us.

The Nautilus blazed forward at top speed with the might of a lunging ram. We reached the surface and waves of clean air flooded the entire ship. I regained consciousness and saw Conseil smiling and shedding a tear for me, we were already on the platform breathing the fine frozen air.

"We must get off this infernal Nautilus," Ned Land said.

CHAPTER 17: FROM CAPE HORN TO THE AMAZON

By April 3, the Nautilus had covered 16,000 leagues. We passed Cape Horn and sped by the shores of Brazil. We took a short break on the waterways of the Amazon on April 11when poor Conseil was attacked by an electric eel.

I laughed, but Conseil was unbelievably frightened. We ate the eel the very next day and the boy learned a lesson: wild things lurk in the water.

CHAPTER 18: THE DEVILFISH

Underneath the Bahamas were sea lilies, star fish, top shell snails, and red tooth snails. The Nautilus sped by caverns in giant underwater cliffs. They belonged to devilfish.

"Devil fish?" Ned Land wondered.

"Master, they are called squid," Conseil said.

"Devilfish," I said, "are no ordinary squid, they're Krake—"

"Kraken!" Ned Land laughed, "fairy tales don't exist. Surely, you don't believe in it professor?"

"It's a legend which has too many first accounts and witnesses of devilfish swallowing small boats."

"The only large squid I can classify is the Bouguer's Squid," Conseil said, "which is 6 meters wide!"

"Ah yes, my boy, the Bouguer's Squid: eight tentacles that move along like snakes and big black eyes. What an awful sight."

Just then a Bouguer's Squid, one10 meters wide swam in our direction. It stared at us with its enormous eye through the window. Its tentacles were twice the length of its body with 250 suckers. It had a beak for a mouth, and it was one of the ugliest things I've ever seen.

Suddenly, the Nautilus stopped moving.

I counted 7 more of them! They were coming out of the caverns in swarms.

"What a strange group of squid," I said.

"Yes," Captain Nemo replied, "and we're going to fight them."

"You can't be serious captain!"

"One tangled up the propeller."

Ned Land overheard and picked up his harpoon. The rest of us grabbed our picks. My mind cowered at the thought of fighting off these devilfish.

The Nautilus surfaced.

The hatch was pulled open by large tentacles! What a scene in front of our eyes as we climbed to the platform! Monsters were slithering up the skirts of the Nautilus.

Captain Nemo chopped through a forest of snake-like tentacles. One of the men was knocked away into the sea with a massive swing. We kept sinking our axes into the flesh of slimy and wretched devilfish.

My heart nearly exploded with excitement and horror. I saw Ned Land out in front thrusting his harpoon at every massive piece of tentacle. Then he stood motionless for a moment and threw it into the largest devilfish's three hearts!

I looked over to Captain Nemo who had tears rolling down his eyes for the man that was lost at sea. I've never experienced such a ferocious battle in my entire life. We fended off these mysterious and horrifying creatures to save the Nautilus.

CHAPTER 19: THE GULF STREAM

After the troubles at sea with the devilfish, we set a course north and entered the Gulf Stream. It's a long and salty river. The current swept along large schools of tiny fish and giant rays that were 7 meters long.

Ned Land had a bout of homesickness.

"It's got to stop, we're heading toward the North Pole," he said.

"But what can we do," I replied.

"We've got to try speaking to Captain Nemo."

"You mean ask the captain if he'll let us off?"

Who was I to stop Ned Land from seeing our precious home land again? And I no longer felt the same enthusiasm after the South Pole accident. I agreed with Ned Land for once, and decided to speak to the captain myself.

"Oh, it's you!" Captain Nemo said.

"Sir, I must speak with you," I insisted, "it's too important for me to wait until you finish."

"What could it be, professor?"

"Will you keep us here forever?" I wondered.

Captain Nemo crossed his arms and without an eye blink he said:

"My answer is the same as it was seven months ago, no one aboard the Nautilus can ever leave."

"But sir, this is slavery!" I shouted.

"Call it what you want," he said, "now let this be the last time we shall talk of this subject. Next time I won't listen."

A storm grew around Long Island as the Nautilus moved by. The propeller hadn't worked since the day it was caught by the terrible devilfish.

In the distant horizon, the storm collapsed homes, roofs, and carried small things in the air. By the end it grew even more. Thunder and lightning appeared in the sky. The Nautilus sank to avoid the dreadful hurricane winds that were wreaking devastation on the surface of the water.

CHAPTER 20: TO EUROPE AGAIN

The Nautilus was thrown east where a long a telegraph cable lay at the bottom of the sea floor 2,800 meters down and led us to Europe again.

Meanwhile, Captain Nemo kept to himself more and more and for days on end. And within Ned Land a dark rage grew.

The Nautilus stopped to make a small detour.

"It's right here! In this exact location!" Captain Nemo said:

The Nautilus sank. There was a massive bulge in the water below us, at least 833 meters.

"This is the Avenger!"

CHAPTER 21: A MASS EXTINCTION

I might never learn of Captain Nemo's history or why he's traveling the sea. The Avenger seemed to be of utter importance to him. He stared at the wreckage. He might have been its captain some time ago. We may never know.

The Nautilus resurfaced. At that moment we felt a huge explosion! I turned to Captain Nemo.

"Captain?"

He didn't reply. I left him in order to find Conseil and Ned Land who were out on the platform .

"What was that explosion, Ned?" I wondered.

"It was a cannon," Ned Land said.

A ship some distance away headed toward the Nautilus. Black smoke was rising from the top of its stacks.

"Arronax," Ned Land warned, "if that battleship gets one mile near us, I'm going to jump overboard, and I suggest you join."

Another explosion blew water hundreds of feet into the air!

"They're firing at us!" I yelled.

"Good lord!" Ned Land shouted.

"They've discovered the narwhal master," Conseil said.

Ned Land waved a white handkerchief into the air.

Captain Nemo appeared and grabbed Ned Land by the shoulders. His eyes were almost shut and he was in a steaming anger, and his was pale.

"Scum!" Captain Nemo yelled, "do you want to be captured?"

He threw Ned down then turned toward the battleship and shouted:

"O ship of a terrible nation, you know who I am! I don't need your colors but I'll show you mine!"

He unrolled a flag, it was black with a golden "N" stitched on the center.

"Go below!" Captain Nemo commanded, "go below now!"

"Captain, are you going to attack the ship?" I asked him.

"I'm going to sink it," he said.

"From what country is that ship, captain?" I wondered.

"If you do not already know then it should be kept from you."

The battleship chased the Nautilus, shooting its ballistic cannons but never hitting.

"There is the ship that I hate! It has taken everything I've ever known, my homeland, my wife, children, father and mother!" Captain Nemo yelled as he steered.

The crewmen began clearing the decks to prepare for an attack.

We made our way to the library where we might be safe from the fearsome machine's cannon balls. Conseil was calm, Ned Land patient, and I was so nervous I shivered, and couldn't hold still.

The Nautilus used the instrument attached to the front of its nose and drove it through the bottom of the battleship, cutting the hard metal in half. Ten meters away I could see water rushing into the massive battleship; the sound was louder than thunder. The water was rising inside of it.

I remained in a state of panic and frozen with fear. The hairs on every part of my body were standing up and my eyes popped out of my head! I saw the battleship's end.

The dark mass of the damaged ship disappeared to the bottom of the sea floor along with its passengers. I turned to Captain Nemo who fell onto his knees, and cried louder than anyone I've ever heard.

I realized that he must use the Nautilus in schemes of vengeance. It's the single explanation of the injured crewman we buried.

CHAPTER 22: THE LAST WORDS OF CAPTAIN NEMO

The deed had been done and not a single soul had taken responsibility. Captain Nemo's actions filled me with horror. The Nautilus was traveling the North Atlantic near England, and I saw not one crewman or the captain around.

"We're going to escape! No one seems to be watching out on the decks or platforms." Ned Land said frantically.

"When?"

"Tonight," he said, "there's land nearby."

"We have no other choice," I said.

There was no question left in my mind of whether or not we should escape. I refused to be the prisoner of a man like Captain Nemo.

Outside of the captain's room I listened. My heart raced, I heard him pace back and forth. He must have not gone to bed for days. All of the past events flashed before my eyes, the Abraham Lincoln, our first boarding of the Nautilus, the underwater strolls, pearl diving, the coral reefs, and the South Pole.

Captain Nemo was not a man anymore in my vision; he was a spirit, the Spirit of the Seas. He lives, he eats, he drinks, and he travels by the sea, never setting afoot on land. He commands the water like a president commands his nation.

It was 9:30 and the night seemed quiet. It was time to make our escape. Captain Nemo left his room and entered the lounge.

My heart raced and pounded as I walked in front of the lounged and Captain Nemo on my way to the longboat.

He came toward me as a ghost. His chest was tight, and he was sobbing. He had not seen me in his stupor of madness.

"O almighty! Enough! Enough!" Captain Nemo yelled out.

I hurried passed him, through the library and reached the room with the longboat. Conseil and Ned Land had been waiting.

"Let's get out of here!" I shouted.

"Right away," Ned Land said.

We boarded the longboat, and then we heard the crew running about loudly.

"Have they discovered us?" I wondered.

"No, listen," Ned Land said softly.

We heard cries that kept on repeating, endlessly. Then an alarm sounded off.

"Whirlpool! Whirlpool! Whirlpool! Whirlpool—"

"Being discovered is the least of our worries now, master," Conseil said.

The Nautilus was traveling near the Norwegian coast line. Here the waters are dangerous. Whirlpools could sink any sized whale even the Nautilus. We were sent this direction either by accident or by the captain himself.

I could feel the Nautilus whirling. I was dizzy and nauseous. The entire ship rocked. Its steel was cracking.

"We've got to hold on tight," Ned Land said.

The waves caught us and ripped the longboat away in a violent thrust. My head hit a wooden post and I lost consciousness. We were dragged into the center of the largest whirlpool in the sea.

CONCLUSION

How we escaped the violent waves that sucked the largest ships and whales in the world, I cannot say. But when I regained consciousness, I was laying inside of a fisherman's hut, and an island somewhere near Norway. Ned Land and Conseil were beside my bed, holding my hand. We smiled at one another. The journey had finally come to an end.

The adventures I have written about were true, and as accurate as possible. But will anyone believe me that I traversed 20,000 leagues under the sea? We experienced the entire world through a sea creature's perspective. We were in the Pacific, the Indian Ocean, the Red Sea, the Mediterranean, the Atlantic, the South Pole, the Arctic waters, and even more north..

My last thoughts remain with the Nautilus and its commander. What became of them? No one may ever see them again, and maybe I shall never learn of his full name or the nation that he hates. I remember him simply as Captain Nemo, the Spirit of the Seas, who explored its greatest depths and I am a witness to the hidden secrets of the earth's vast body of water.

END

26791721R00072

Made in the USA
Middletown, DE
06 December 2015